What I Should Have Done: Stories

Marlys Addison

Bishop Publishing

DEDICATION

This effort is dedicated to my mother, who enabled my reading habit and who thinks I'm pretty great.

CONTENTS

ACKNOWLEDGEMENT

No big project is created alone. I couldn't write if my family, friends, coworkers, and acquaintances hadn't been such rich, engaging people.

Please Say Yes

I asked him to please not do this until he knew for sure. Maybe he misunderstood me and thought I was saying he shouldn't ask until *he* was sure *he* wanted to get married. But what I meant was I didn't want him to ask until he was sure *I* wanted to get married. Maybe I should have been clearer. That may seem crazy, or at least unromantic, but if a couple can't talk about when and if they want to get engaged, then should they really be getting engaged?

I mean, sure, it's nice if when and how are a surprise; that is where the man gets to be creative and gets to be a man and feel like he is in control and making this decision for himself. For them. He also gets a bit of that when he decides what type of and how big of a ring to buy. I would think that would be enough.

But some men want to have complete control and they want to spring the question without talking to their girlfriend. I think they are either risk-takers or very confident men who could never imagine a woman telling them no.

I think my boyfriend, Brett, falls into the latter group; he was just so confident in our love that he never imagined I meant what I said when I told him to talk to me before doing anything, "life changing." Knowing him like I do, I think he figured I was just trying to be super-controlling and wanted to control a situation that he, like most men, feels should be controlled by the man.

The control issue isn't exactly right in this case. I mean, I do like to control things and the fact is that things usually go well when I'm in control. But the control thing truly wasn't the issue this time. This time I was just trying to save everyone involved a lot of heartache.

And boy are there a lot of people involved. We

met at work, where we work in a violent environment and friendships, loves, and hate-ships develop quickly, are strong, and last a long time. Lots of married couples and lots of people who hate each other or would die for each other. So, even though he is security and I am education, my friends are his friends and his friends are my friends. People like us; they think we match; they want to see us together.

And our families too. My family loves him. My nephew wants to be him. My mom thinks he's my salvation, which is a pretty big deal since she would be just as happy if I were a single, angry, feminist my entire life.

So, all these people are emotionally invested in our relationship and are affected by our decisions. Let alone our own emotions. This is no faint-hearted romance.

We liked each other from a far and had an intense professional relationship before we could both manage to be single at the same time. Then he got deployed and we waited for each other. Fourteen months of phone calls only. Phone calls every night, making us lucky, to be sure, but just phone calls all the same. Fourteen months of planning our entire days around when we could talk. Fourteen months of being alone but not being available.

Fourteen months of waiting. Waiting to start a new life. Waiting to see if we actually get along in person on a romantic level. Fourteen months of waiting to see if we mesh sexually. Fourteen months of going everywhere stag. Fourteen months of missing each other horribly.

Everyone was sure he would propose when he came home on leave. But he was too smart for that and I had faith in that intelligence, enough that I never even warned him not to propose. And he didn't. You don't propose four months into a relationship because you're on leave and it would be romantic.

Being the sexist society we live in, people assumed I was disappointed both times he came home and we didn't get engaged. I didn't even waste my breath telling people that I didn't want to get engaged while he was deployed. Too cliché. And given our situation, too irresponsible.

And when he got home, everyone again assumed we would get engaged quickly. But again, we were too smart for that. We hadn't been together for more than five weeks of our entire fifteen month long relationship. Too soon.

And then we moved in together and even though I

started to have doubts before he got home about the intelligence of this plan, I didn't back out, it seemed too negative. So we moved in together and it was even worse than I had imagined. Everything was off, everything was wrong.

So at that time I was actually *glad* we weren't engaged. I would've felt trapped. As bad as some people see living in sin, that was the best option for me (aside from us not living together at all, which was no longer an option). And as horrible as this may seem, I was glad I had time to decide if he was right for me. I had time to decide if this relationship was right for me. Yes, we had signed a lease, but there is nothing permanent about a lease. I had a huge and total out. And even though I didn't want to think that he might be feeling this way, I knew that *he* had an out, too.

So, I was getting pretty comfortable with the idea of us living together and seeing if we could make this work with both of us having an out. I was settling in. I was feeling calm enough to make decisions.

And then Valentine's Day came. Never in a million years would I think he would be cliché enough to propose on Valentine's. After passing all the cliché's of proposing while he was deployed, he fell for the biggest one of all?

And in falling for this damned Valentine's Day cliché, he forced me into a decision. A decision I had hoped not to have to make.

But I loved and respected this man, so I sat there thinking about how those facts did indeed require me to seriously consider his request. Even if I didn't want to.

So I started thinking about what life with him had been like so far. I thought about all the laughs we have had, I thought about all the great work we have done for the juvenile inmates at the facility we work at, I thought about the fact that he sometimes massages my back for no reason, I thought about how we like to go see movies, I thought about how he'll come with me to the library and the bookstore. I thought about how he is respectful to me and nice to my family. I thought about how everyone he meets loves him. I thought about how handsome he is. I thought about what a hard-worker he is and how responsible he is with his money. I thought about how good he is with my dog.

And then I started imaging what life would be like when we were married. I thought about how he never has enough energy to walk my dog. I thought about how he is so dedicated to work that he often doesn't have time for me. I thought about how his moral code sometimes makes him seem like a goody-two shoes. I thought about how he is friends with everyone and is so friendly that sometimes females might think he is coming on to them. I thought about how he only massages my back after he's done something to make me mad. And I thought about how he never massages my legs at all. And I thought about how he will probably always work holidays. I thought about how he is so big that our kids would probably tear me in half. I thought about how he leaves pants and shoes on the living room floor for an entire week, but then cleans so thoroughly on Sundays that I feel like a schlep. I thought about how I probably wouldn't enjoy taking care of an able-bodied adult for the rest of her life.

I thought of all these things while I starred at his wonderful, handsome face. Soon I realized that there is a point where silence becomes an answer in and of itself. I realized when his beautiful face went from sheer joy and excitement, to questioning, to a pleading, "please say yes" look, and finally to heartbroken recognition. I leaned over to kiss Brett on the cheek and then got up and left the restaurant. I left much more than a half-finished meal and an unpaid bill behind.

Mistakes

Julie

There are moments in every person's life where you have to make decisions. Well, this is basically every single day! Tall or grande? Double or triple? Speed or get there late? Take a moment out to talk to that coworker, or just go on with your day? Most of these seem rather small, but they add up. One hundred calories here. Extra energy there. The occasional speeding ticket. Earning a label of "nice" at work. Yes, these little decisions *are* important. But this story is really about decisions that, while maybe not life altering decision, do have a larger effect on your life then say putting on 10 pounds every year because you absolutely have to have a that grande.

***

This wasn't the way we had planned it. And we *had* planned it. Meaning we had actually talked about it, come to a shared conclusion we were both comfortable with and then, I thought, put a pin in it. Apparently not. I had been dating Steve for about three months at the point of departure from the plan. Not a very long time at all, really.

But it was obvious we really liked each other and were exclusive. We had really only one or two things in common. We both like to travel and we were both into running, cycling, and triathlons. But that's not a ton of things in common and Steve's life was a mess. Just a complete and utter mess. He was only recently divorced from his wife of almost 15 years. I didn't realize how recently until after we already started dating. Continuing to date him at this point- mistake one. They had two kids together and he had fought hard for shared custody. He assured me when we met that all the legal battles were over. He didn't realize at the time that he was wrong. Continuing to date Steve after the legal battles started back up, mistake two.

But my story is really about mistake three- which I'll get to in a minute.

A few weeks after we met, Steve's ex-wife decided she wanted full custody of their kids, rather than to split custody 60/40. The day after their divorce was final, this woman married the man she left Steve for. And a week after their custody battle was closed, she reopened it. It came out later that her new husband didn't want Steve so involved in the lives of his "new" children. These two were a dream couple, to be sure. Steve, already a good guy and, apparently, a good father, kicked it into over drive. He was going above and beyond. Partly because he saw that might lose his sons, but also because it knew his ex-wife had become a lazy parent. He wanted to be ready for custody battle that might fall along the lines of who is the better, more involved parent.

That meant we saw even less of each other than our busy schedules already allowed. We had agreed that I wouldn't be introduced to his sons until we were sure we were serious. Once the custody battle started, that became even more important.

I was totally okay with that. As a girl, I was more than excited to know that I would always know where I stood in our relationship. Additionally, since I was Steve's first relationship since his divorce, I was well aware that I might be a rebound and I didn't want to get too involved. Finally, I wasn't sure where I stood on the matter of becoming an instant stepmom. I wasn't even sure I wanted kids, let alone wanted to have to help raise someone else's kids. Especially since Steve's ex seemed so extreme and crazy. I wasn't ready to sign on to have this woman have partial control of the rest of my life. I didn't know I would ever be ready for that, let alone after we'd been dating a short three months. So, a long lead time on meeting Steve's sons was totally fine with me.

But, less than a week after we reaffirmed this, Steve asked me to have dinner with his sons. This is where mistake three started.

I checked my phone during lunch and saw a text from Steve. He was inviting me out to dinner that night. I thought it was a bit weird that he'd asked because he was supposed to have his sons that night. But I texted an acceptance and went on with my day.

It was the last day of school before winter break and I was out at happy hour with some coworkers. I had nothing to do, my training was in a slow-down phase, and I just had time to drink and hang out. A rarity for a triathlete with two jobs!

As I listened to my coworkers share their stories of worst dates ever, I got a phone call from Steve. I was tempted not to answer, to just call him back after the bar. I should have ignored because he was calling to tell me that he did has his sons that night. And he still wanted to have dinner.

The mistake was in not questioning him. Why had he changed his mind so quickly about me meeting his sons? Or had he all of a sudden, within a week, decided we'd moved from dating to super serious? And why didn't he leave time to talk about this so I could break it to him that I wasn't feeling we were quite that serious? Because I wasn't. I liked him and all, but I had all those reservations about getting involved in his messy, messy life.

I didn't want to become a person who "relationship embellishes." This is when one of the people in the relationship has some major issue and the couple decides to date anyway. Because of the issues, they don't do all the proper relationship- building stuff. But they do keep dating. And they count all the complications they experience as obstacles they "make it through" and time "in." It becomes a situation where they don't really have a strong relationship, but they think they do. The longer the complications in the one partner's life lasts, the longer they go on not developing a full relationship but thinking they have a strong one. And if those complications ever disappear, well, then the couple is left with a less-than-full relationship. Some couples can make it through that and move back to the relationship-building stage, but most can't.

So I didn't want to meet his sons that night, but I didn't tell Steve that. Instead I got off the phone with Steve and told my coworker and friend, Michael, that I didn't want to meet Steve's sons. As a true guy, he told me to, "just tell Steve." Riiiight. I'll get right on that.

I ended up going to dinner that night. We shared a loud, sticky, wet, disturbing meal at a Red Robin, which I had never realized was so "family friendly." I haven't eaten at a Red Robin since. And, needless to say, Steve and I are no longer dating.

We dated another six weeks. I ended up spending Christmas evening with him- and his sons. I went sledding with his sons over Christmas Break. Then I met his father on New Years. But all during that time, things were changing. I am a total wimp, apparently a person who cannot tell someone they aren't ready to meet their sons, but I am not a quitter. So since Steve and I had agreed that meeting his sons would single a turning point in our relationship, I jumped in fully, if not reluctantly, to the role of devoted girlfriend and potentially future stepmom.

But while I was trying to fulfill that role, Steve was pulling back. He was busier at work. He didn't have time for group workouts like he used to. At first I barely noticed his withdraw because I was busy working, training, and trying to calm my nerves about the decision I had made.

When we finally had "the talk" it was friendly enough, although I did yell at him for confusing me. I should have been yelling at myself. I should have listened to my gut. I accepted Steve's invite to dinner that December night because I was afraid he might be so offended by my refusal that it might damage or even end our relationship. And I was more afraid of that than of what might happen if I did meet his sons. The only problem is that we broke up anyway and the last six weeks our relationship weren't as great as they could have been.

Not following my gut is *my mistake.*

Mary

I met Jeremy at a marathon. My girlfriend, Jen, was running and I was there to support her. She had given a list of places on the 26.2 mile course where people could easily pull off the road and get out and watch and cheer friends on. Jen, in her typical Type A personality, had not only notified us these locations, but she had assigned us posts. Her sister, Sammy got mile 5. Jen's coworker got mile 12. I got mile 18. Her husband got the finish line.

Apparently a lot of people had this idea, because I was joined by at least twenty other supporters. Thousands of people were running this marathon and they all hard varying paces, and most of those people had wide margins of error, especially by mile 18. Someone who is planning on running their marathon in about 3 hours would be running about 7 minute miles, meaning they would be passing the 18 mile mark in about 2 hours and 6 minutes. But a lot can happen in 18 miles, so I got to the cheerleading point when the Jen had only been running about 90 minutes.

Family and friends of racers were lined up along a quarter mile stretch of a grassy road. I had my phone and a book and I was getting ready to just sit back and wait.

But instead I was drawn into a conversation with a large group of people. We talked about our friends and family and our own lives.

Over all it was a great afternoon and we ended up cheering for everyone who passed, not just our own family and friends. While we were talking, I noticed a blond guy making a point of talking to me. I wasn't sure what I thought of him, but it didn't matter because I wanted to try to get to the finish line, even if I didn't have strict orders to do so.

As it turned out, the blond, Jeremy, was at the finish line, too. Miles 18-26 take a bit of time, so even with having to drive, park, and walk to the finish line, Jeremy and I plenty of time to talk once we bumped into each other near the finish line.

His friend came into the finish line about twenty-five minutes before Jen did, but before Jeremy left to tend to this friend, he asked me out to dinner for that night.

I agreed, even on such short notice, because Jeremy told me he and his friend Mark were serving on the military base 250 miles away. They had plans to stay the night in town and then they would drive back the next morning.

***

We had a great dinner. We laughed like kids. He reminded me of my childhood family friend, Dale. We laughed and had a great time, but I wasn't sure how attracted I was to Jeremy. He was barely taller than me and not much bigger. I wasn't running any marathons, but I was in ok shape. So a man being almost my size, meant he was small, or least smaller than I typically like. Also, I found out Jeremy was 26 to my 29 years old. Not a huge difference, but when you come to men and women and relationships, that can be a huge difference. Men are already pretty immature. So, I wasn't super happy to maybe date a younger guy.

But at 29 I was starting to wonder if maybe I had been too picky in the past. Maybe happiness is happiness? So I was willing to go to that dinner. And I was willing to go to dinner with Jeremy the next weekend when he came into town. And the next weekend.

We always laughed together and we had a good time together. The age issue didn't seem to come up very often and I was greatly flattered that he kept driving 500 miles a weekend to have dinner with me. And while he made apparent he was interested in my physically, he never pressured me to stay over in his hotel room.

But a few kissing sessions in his hotel room was not enough to really get the fires burning and I was starting to think maybe we would just be friends. And I can't say I was against that. While he hadn't pressured me to stay overnight in his hotel, I hadn't pushed myself on him either.

And then things changed when he started asking me to come down to him instead of him coming to me. He said he would pay for the hotel room. It didn't take long for that situation to turn into him staying over at the hotel. Still though, nothing materialized. We were on the fast track to friendship.

This lasted for months, a relationship not really going anywhere but me being committed and potentially missing other people and relationships.

Eventually we just stopped hanging out. One weekend I was busy, another weekend he was busy and before long we just petered out.

No big deal, but I wasted a few months in a relationship that I knew from the start was not going anywhere.

My mistake, trying to make something out of nothing.

Lou Ellen

I met Seth at a party at a friend's house. I was immediately drawn to him. His tall, full frame, and his healthy butt, were all attractive to me immediately. And we had a lot in common, too. We were both free spirits. He liked to meditate and we actually meditated the morning after we met. Some said we moved too quickly. But I felt more comfortable with him than I had ever felt with anyone.

Within two months I was practically living at his apartment. Within six months we found a place together. We hosted great parties, we adopted a puppy, and we mourned the death of my cat. We were the envy of our friends (at least mine). But we never seemed to progress beyond there. I started dating Seth when I was twenty-four years old. At that time, I was happy to have a great boyfriend and relationship. But by the time I was thirty, that set up was getting tired. I wasn't fulfilled anymore. I was ready for marriage and Seth just wasn't there.

We went round and round the issue for almost a

year before we decided to part ways. We tried to part ways amicably. We remained friends and I even went to his house-warming when he moved in with our mutual friend Shelly. They moved in together less than three months after we broke up. Three months and they were not only dating, but living together.

That house-warming party was probably one of the worst experiences of my life. I was trying so hard to actually be okay with my ex of six years moving on so quickly, and with a *friend*. I wanted so badly to be okay with the situation that I told my friends I was okay with this. I invited them to Seth's house-warming and when they all seemed hesitant; I convinced them it was fine.

It was absolutely not fine. It was so awkward. Seth and Shelly were renting an amazing house, for way more money than Seth had ever been willing to spend on our rentals. And since they were still newly dating, they were in that goofy, fun, all-over-each-other stage. But because Shelly had been our friend, she and Seth knew each other. So they had a bond and comfortableness that was obvious to everyone. Especially my friends.

My ever-faithful friends were pissed by the entire experience. They felt that Shelly and Seth had probably had something before we officially broke up. I tried to convince them they were wrong, but the longer the night went on, the more unlikely that seemed.

By the end of the night, I felt horrible. I was sure Seth and Shelly had been cheating on me before we broke up and I felt I had subjected my friends to an unfair situation where I brought them into the lion's den and then asked them not to be pissed on my behalf.

That entire party, forcing my friends into that situation, is *my biggest mistake*.

Her Calendar Disappeared

Her calendar disappeared. She unlocked her phone and it was gone. Frantic searching; May, April, March. This happened to her friend. Did Sal's calendar come back? She never asked. Was this a Mac-thing; should she reboot?

Days passed, obligations were missed. She had an excuse, "My calendar disappeared, I'm so jumbled!"

There were things she could remember, but she didn't put them back on the calendar. Birthdays, annual events, family get-togethers. She'd relist the really important things…tomorrow. She'd remember on her own what really matters, she thought.

She didn't add anything. Not anniversaries, meetings, nor recurring To-Dos. She felt free, more liberated than she'd felt since before she got married.

She didn't reboot.

What I Should Have Done

My funeral was attended by many people, but not as many and not the ones I would have liked. Of course my family was there: my mother, my sisters and their husbands and children. All the Johnsons were there, with wives and girlfriends in tow. Even a few long-lost friends were there.

The ones who were missing were the ones who led me to my death. My closest friends played a part, but they never meant to. I don't want them to think about their role and feel bad, so it makes me happy to know that as time passes, they will think less and less of me. Their lives will go on while I lie in the ground. But, certain things will always remind them of me.

For Molly, it will be driving past the mortuary on her way home from work. Remembering me will make Molly sad, because she will think there was something she could have done to stop my life from ending up here, in the ground.

During the 80s and 90s I was living high, literally and figuratively. I joined the Navy right after high school. I had girlfriends, I had tons of great friends, and I had time and money to do what I wanted. My father had not yet lost all his money so I could still get whatever I wanted from him. And what I wanted was fun, drugs, sex, adventure, and girls. Girls and sex where mutually exclusive for me. Some girls were for sex, plain and simple. I often didn't even know their names and I never stayed long after I had sex with them. Other girls were friends, and sex was off-limits. We would flirt and pet and kiss, and hang out, but they never wanted more from me. They would go home to their own beds and their boyfriends at night, even if they spent the better part of the evening hanging all over my dick. I liked the attention I would get from these girls. And even though they were doing this with all my friends it still felt nice and I didn't care. And between us guys we kept it cool. No one got jealous if, for instance, Tina would go on and on about how big Kale's cock was, and the next minute be in our lap. Kale would know that he had gotten his and I would be fine knowing that she would touch me, kiss me, give me a hand job, maybe a blow job, and that would be all I would need from her. I was probably the only one among my buddies who wasn't fucking these "friends" of ours, but like I said, I was getting it somewhere else. These girls were about ego for me.

The Johnsons felt especially guilty after my death. We had been so close all through childhood that they felt that the way we grew apart was their fault. They thought they should have made more of an effort to call, to invite me to family get-togethers, or to the movies. But it wasn't their fault because we didn't grow apart as much as that they grew up and I never did. While they went out and grabbed life and opportunities, I continued on the same path, let good things pass me by. I just couldn't adjust. The girls I used to hang out with got older, got fatter, got pregnant, got married. And the girls who took their places (and there were always girls, because there are always girls willing to have a good time for some attention) weren't the same. They didn't grab my attention at all, or they wanted more from me than I could give. So yeah, there were still girls, but they were fewer and less exciting.

And to make things worse, the guys were changing too. Kirk had been married for almost ten years when I died. Kevin was on and- off-again engaged to a girl that had stuck by him through all the cheating. I guess a six-figure salary will get you that type of loyalty. Kenny married the girl he knocked up on their first date. Of course they got a divorce, but even after that he pretty much always had a girl around. But me, I just couldn't put it all together. But I can't complain because I had my chance.

My big chance, the one I totally screwed up, was with Molly. I met her because she rented a room from Kenny. I was doing some work in the backyard when she came home from work one day. She found me all sweaty, shirt off, in her backyard and instead of flirting with me she asked me who I was and whether authorized to be working back there. She was so unlike all of us, a bit of a bore, really.

Molly was a librarian and she managed her own library. I mean, a *librarian*. I should have known. Librarians seem boring and she lived up to that stereotype because even though she was ten years younger than us, she *acted* like she was ten years older than us. She could be boring, but she was really funny too. And she wasn't a classic beauty like the girls I would imagine marrying someday, and she wasn't smoking hot like the girls I usually fucked, but she was alluring in her own unusual way. She wasn't my type at all, but something just drew me to her.

I couldn't figure out how to deal with her. I found myself asking her on dates, like to go golfing or whatever. And since she wasn't the typical beauty and because she was younger, I figured she would be excited to even be asked. Instead, she acted like she couldn't really care. And then halfway through our first date (hole nine) she asked me to hurry up!

After that date she didn't even call me, which girls normally do. I didn't even hear from her again until I went to pick Kenny one night. Typical Molly, it was nine at night and she was already in her glasses and pajamas. Something about the way she really didn't seem to care that she hadn't heard from me and that I wasn't there for her made me want her even more. I wanted to take her out with us and show her what her life with me would be like. But she told me she was "good" and "in for the night" when I asked.

That was it; this woman had so completely taken my attention that she was all I could think about. I started to do volunteer jobs around the house for Kenny's mom just so I could be around Molly. I knew she got home from work around four, so I would make sure to be out back, shirt off and sweaty about that time.

Most times she would totally ignore me and sit down and do work, read a book, or watch television. But, sometimes she would bring me out a beer and talk to me while I worked. So, I was pretty sure she was interested too, but she acted so differently than the girls I was used to. I just couldn't figure her out.

I knew I had to ask her out again, and I knew that my regular haunts would not work for her. So, we went for drives, we ran errands together, I helped her make, copy, and distribute flyers of her dog when he ran away, we met at bars that were a little less sleazy than my regular hangouts. In just a few weeks, I realized I really liked Molly. I felt no need to have sex with her and just leave. I felt no need to pressure her to do something sexual for me and then ignore her. In fact, at this point I hadn't even kissed her. I was starting to see what my committed friends found alluring about that set up. And my friends, who really liked the idea of me with Molly, teased me about that to no end.

"If you don't want it, I I'll take it!"

"What are you waiting for, for her to make the first move?"

Most of the comments were joking and I blew them off, but one comment Kenny made shocked me. He told me that Molly was not the type of girl to make the first move and no wonder she was seeing someone else.

What? *What*! I'm laying my heart on the line here and Molly was seeing someone else? And after questioning Kenny I found out that this guy was like four years older than me, which made him *way* older than Molly, and he was also short and chubby. What could she possibly want with a guy like that when she could have a guy like me?

Now, normally, I would have left the situation all together; forgotten about Molly totally. And I honestly tried. I started going back to the bars where the whores were and I would be a total ass to Molly when I came to pick up Kenny. The girls even rewarded my return with extra attention. But I just couldn't get into it. All I could think about was Molly being out with the old guy. It drove me crazy.

So, I did what I had never done up to that point. I

made the drunk, two in the morning phone call. When Molly answered I asked her where she was, if she was out with the old guy. Molly hadn't realized that I knew about the old guy, but she put it all together very quickly. But she didn't seem upset to be caught at all. She simply said, "He and I haven't done anything, and neither have we, Jonah. I thought you might like me, and I like you, but I'm not your typical type and since you haven't made any moves, I figured you were looking for a friendship."

"I do want a friendship, but I want more. I want to touch you, hold you, make love to you. I want to *be* with you, Molly." Oh shit, not good. I practically just proposed to this chick and I haven't even kissed her! I hung up on Molly and knew I had to do some damage control or I would have to avoid her for weeks to erase the possible effects of what I just said. Drunk as a motherfucker, I speed over to Kenny's house. I hadn't thought about the door being locked and when I didn't see Kenny's car, I figured I might have wasted a trip.

"What the fuck, fucker?" Molly screamed at me when she finally opened the door after leaving me to knock for almost five. "Call and wake me up to say stupid things. Way to be fucking sincere! Asshole!"

I realized at this point that I had upset Molly. I realized that I probably did mean what I had said earlier, and I realized that treating her like all the whores I usually hung out with wasn't fair, and that she obviously wouldn't stand for it. I started to wonder where a girl who was so…average could have gotten the nerve to stand up for herself like that. Most girls had never been able to resist me. Molly slammed her door in my face and I took that as my cue to leave.

I tossed and turned all night and as soon as I felt it was decent to do so, I called Molly and asked if she would let me buy her a cup of coffee. To my surprise, she agreed. I picked her and her dog up and we drove in silence to Satellite coffee shop on Rio Grande. I ordered our coffees while she found us a seat outside and hitched her dog to the latch near the table. We sat in silence for a few minutes after I sat down. Finally I couldn't stand it anymore, so I started.

"Look, Molly, I really like you and all. I guess things just keep getting messed up." I knew I was still skirting the issue, definitely not taking responsibility for my actions, but it was all I could give. But thankfully Molly jumped right in to save me from myself.

"Look, Jonah, let me tell you something about me. I *need* very few things in a man. The biggest thing is, I need to be able to *admire* the man I am with. Sometimes I think you are a great guy, but other times I cannot understand you. You were in the military, I can admire that. But when you tell stories about that time, they are all about drinking, which is a little lame. And they are also all about how you hated all the people in all the countries you traveled to. I cannot admire that. It's so…immature *and* I want to travel if I ever have the money to, but you act like you wouldn't enjoy going. Also, money. You are smart and you have training, but you can't seem to hold down a job. I find that incredibly lazy, and I cannot admire that. Also, if I ever had the time to travel, I would need a guy who could at least pay his half. That doesn't seem to describe you. Also, your car. You drove me here in a nice truck, which you have essentially stolen. You *bragged* to me that you haven't made a payment in eight months. Did you think that would impress me? Because it doesn't. You're stealing, and I can't admire that. You are funny and I am attracted to you physically. I mean *really* attracted. I think about you at night. I *want* more than you can imagine to be with you, to call you my boyfriend, but I'm guarded because I don't think you are the type to have girlfriends. And that's another thing; don't give me shit for dating someone else when you are the one who is actually whoring around. Okay, I'm done. You may talk now."

I was floored. I couldn't believe that she had called me out like that. I couldn't believe that she had called me out so accurately. And, I couldn't believe she had had the nerve to lay her cards on the table, when I still hadn't. I committed right then and there to myself that I would be with Molly no matter what it took.

We made a date to play pool and have drinks at her favorite bar that night. I went home and took a nap because I wanted to make this the first night we had sex. When I got up I started in on cleaning the house. I put out candles for later that night and extra towels for the next morning. But as the day wore on, I started to get nervous, to feel edgy. By the time nine-thirty rolled around, I found myself in a bar down the street from Anodyne, where I was supposed to meet Molly.

I knew I had some leeway because Molly was there with friends playing pool, but really, my point was to be as late as I possible could without her calling the whole thing off. I don't know why I was doing this to her, but I couldn't help myself.

When I finally showed up to Anodyne, Molly was having a great time with her friends, and they didn't skip a beat. They were all a little slap-happy and my being late without an explanation didn't seem to bother them a bit. Fuck! I am not sure what I was going for, but it certainly wasn't nobody caring. In fact, Molly was more approachable and inviting than she had ever been. She was in one of those places where you just feel safe and happy and nothing can get in your way. I envied her, because I was definitely not there. I hadn't had sex with a person I actually cared about for years, and I was nervous about what it would be like in the morning.

Turns out, I didn't need to worry. I ordered a round of beers and we all played a few more games of pool, and then Molly and I begged off and headed for my house. When we got to my house I set a fire and opened the bottle of wine I bought for the occasion. We drank it and made light conversation.

We finished the wine, and it was becoming obvious that we would have to move to the next room. And we did. We moved into my room and started to make out on the bed. My god, she felt wonderful to the touch! I would have never thought that someone so...average could feel this good. But, something was wrong. When it was time to make the final commitment, I couldn't. It was obvious she was willing and I just couldn't. At first, I was totally hard, ready to be inside of her, but I just couldn't bring myself to take my pants off. Then I just couldn't keep it up. And believe me, this had never happened before.

It didn't take Molly long to figure out something was wrong. I had to do something, so I excused myself to the restroom, but instead I went in the opposite direction to the kitchen. I was shaking while I made a turkey sandwich, poured myself some soda, walked into the living room and sat down. Molly waited until it was obvious that I had not gone to the bathroom and then she ambushed me.

"Is something wrong?" Her voice sounded so pleading and small, vulnerable, nothing like Molly. I felt sick to my stomach to be doing this to her, especially since I knew I would never tell her why this was happening.

"Nah, I just didn't eat dinner and I got really hungry all of a sudden. I want to be able to give you my all when we finally do it." Lame, I know. And *she* knew. But she went back to the bedroom, presumably to sleep, but I'm sure I heard her crying.

I never went back to that bed that night. I slept on the undersized couch. Actually, I hardly slept, and I know Molly was tossing and turning all night too. But I never went back in there and she never came back out. Until morning, that is. By then she was so enraged that I was actually a little fearful.

"Wake up and take me home, Jonah," she demanded as she pounded my arm. I ignored her for as long as I could. Then, when it was obvious that I was awake, I asked her if she could just take a cab. That was a good one, huh! I mean, officially I felt horrible, but I had committed to this horrible line.

"No, I won't take a cab. But I will take your truck if you don't get up in about ten seconds and take me yourself you lazy bastard." I believed her for many reasons, but mostly because she had been faster than me in making for my keys, which she now held firmly in her hand.

"Fine, fine," I mumbled as I put my shoes on.

We drove to her and Kenny's place in silence, right until the end when I told her that I hoped she felt bad because I had a cramp in my calf from sleeping on the couch and that I would blame her if I couldn't play golf later that day. That was a bit much, even for me. I actually saw the tough exterior of Molly erupt into something besides anger, something that was so unusual for Molly that I almost didn't recognize it; sadness.

I rarely saw Molly after that, but I thought about her all the time. I couldn't figure out why I hadn't been able to perform, but I did finally come to realize why I was so mean to her afterwards. For whatever reason, I couldn't perform for a girl that should have been begging me for it. In fact, Molly threw everything in my life off kilter and then I was the one who couldn't get it done. I was angry at her for putting me in that position in the first place. But, like I said, that didn't mean I stopped thinking about her.

I never met another girl like her; no girl ever made me want to try, no girl ever made me unable to perform, no girl ever even surprised me, and no girl threw me off balance and made me feel like shit for the way I act like Molly had. In fact, a few years later we ran into each other at a going away party for Kenny. As usual, I was broke because I hadn't worked in a few months. But still, I ordered the drinks and food I wanted, thinking that someone would just pick up the check like usual. But this time, for some reason, everyone split out their bill. I was saddled with a $30 bill, one I could not pay. Everyone got all bent out of shape. Kenny and Kevin were calling me names and telling me to pay, Kirk was trying to calm them down, but still insisting that I pay. About this time Molly got up to leave. She had a smirk on her face, and I could just not stand that.

"Hey, I didn't see Molly lay any money down! What, if you're an uptight bitch you don't have to pay?" My words were poisonous enough, but I pretty much yelled them, drawing attention to all of us in the bar of this fancy restaurant. Molly looked back at me with a sad look in her eyes.

"I'm driving, Jonah. I only had water. I didn't want anything, didn't even want to come except to say goodbye to Kenny. In fact, the guys had to convince me that you could behave yourself for even one hour. I believed them. I guess we were all wrong." And just like that, she walked away. She walked out of my life, forever.

Two months before my death Molly meet my old friend, Kale. By chance, she took a job as the librarian at the school where he was already working as a teacher. They hit it off right away, and only thought it was funny that years ago they had both know the same group of guys.

Molly made no indication to Kale that one of those guys had been more important to her than any of the others. But I know I had been. I know that she often thought back to our time together and regretted that I was such a fuck-up. Molly saw me as that guy "who would have been perfect if only…" Of course, at that time I didn't know that.

Then, after one more drunken Christmas alone, I came to the horrifying realization that these thousands of small fuck-ups had ruined my life. I couldn't go back and fix these things. There hadn't been any women to interest me in years, and even the whores were moving on since I never had money and hadn't been able to perform the same since that disastrous night with Molly. And while I didn't know that Molly and Kale were together, didn't even know if Molly was in the state any more, I knew I could never go back to that. I was so tired of seeing everyone else put their lives together happily, while I couldn't even find a meaningless relationship. I was thirty-eight, single, no kids, no money, no real job, nothing to show for all my hard work or even all my laziness, and I finally just had to give up; it just became too much.

*   *   *

My funeral was held on a cold rainy night in January. As people drove to the mortuary they worried about not being able to see the lines in the road to the dark, wet road. My family was there. The Johnsons were there. The whores weren't there. Molly wasn't there. The people who lead to my death weren't there.

ABOUT THE AUTHOR

Marlys Addison grew up in Albuquerque, New Mexico and has been a teacher for many years in New Mexico, Wisconsin, and Oregon. She has always loved to read and write. She lives with her husband, daughter, and two dogs.